The ONCE UPON AMERICA® Series

# Tough Choices

## A STORY OF THE VIETNAM WAR

### BY NANCY ANTLE

ILLUSTRATED BY MICHELE LAPORTE

VIKING

*Thanks to Mike Gries, a man I chanced to sit beside on an airplane,*
*who turned out to be the son of a Vietnam vet*
*and who got me reading the right books for my research;*
*Gordon Walker, a friend and Vietnam vet,*
*who answered all my questions and critiqued the first draft;*
*and Kay, Doug, and Kate for their invaluable criticism and moral support.*

VIKING
Published by the Penguin Group
Penguin Books USA Inc., 375 Hudson Street, New York, New York 10014, U.S.A.
Penguin Books Ltd, 27 Wrights Lane, London W8 5TZ, England
Penguin Books Australia Ltd, Ringwood, Victoria, Australia
Penguin Books Canada Ltd, 10 Alcorn Avenue, Toronto, Ontario, Canada M4V 3B2
Penguin Books (N.Z.) Ltd, 182–190 Wairau Road, Auckland 10, New Zealand

Penguin Books Ltd, Registered Offices: Harmondsworth, Middlesex, England

First published in 1993 by Viking, a division of Penguin Books USA Inc.

1   3   5   7   9   10   8   6   4   2

**Library of Congress Cataloging-in-Publication Data**
Antle, Nancy.
Tough choices : a story of the Vietnam War / by Nancy Antle ;
illustrated by Michele Laporte.    p.    cm. — (Once upon America)
Summary: Samantha finds herself torn by her loyalty to her two brothers,
one a soldier recently returned from the war in Vietnam and the other a war protester.
I S B N   0 - 6 7 0 - 8 4 8 7 9 - 4
1. Vietnamese Conflict, 1961–1975—Juvenile fiction.
[1. Vietnamese Conflict, 1961–1975—Fiction.   2. Brothers and sisters—Fiction.]
I. Laporte, Michele, ill.   II. Title.   III. Series.
PZ7.A6294To   1993   [Fic]—dc20    93-14871   CIP   AC

*To Lee Utal,*
*the person who believed*
*I would be a writer someday,*
*long before I believed it myself.*
*Thanks, Mom.*

# Contents

# Homecoming

"Hurry up!" I yelled to Mom and the others. I could see the United sign across the airport parking lot.

"Samantha, no one should have to hurry in August," Mom said. I looked back at her. She had stopped to wipe the sweat from her face with a handkerchief.

"So much for makeup," she said. She laughed. "I don't suppose Mitchell would know his mom with makeup on anyway."

Lee Ann Wilkerson stood beside Mom, holding her

arm. Good grief! I thought. Mom wasn't even 40. She didn't need anyone to help her walk.

Everything about Lee Ann Wilkerson bugged me. Her perfectly straight brown hair. Her dumb laugh. And, especially, the fact that my oldest brother was in love with her.

"You hurry if you want to," Emmett added. "I don't want to pass out just so I can see G.I. Joe sooner."

Lee Ann turned around and hit him in the stomach with her purse.

"What did you do that for?" Emmett asked. As if he didn't know.

"I'll hit you with my purse next, if you don't keep quiet," Mom said.

"It's a free country," Emmett said. In the fall, he was going to be a junior in high school. But he sure sounded stupid sometimes.

"Emmett, you promised," I said.

He looked at me and frowned. He pushed a strand of blond hair out of his eyes.

"Okay, okay," he said. "I said I wouldn't argue with Mitch about the war *today*. I'll keep my promise."

I frowned back at him. I'd never forgive him if he ruined Mitch's homecoming. Mitch had been gone for over a year fighting in the war in Vietnam. He had a month off now. Then he had to report to a base in North Carolina. I wanted his time at home to be happy.

I twisted the silver bracelet on my wrist while I

waited for Mom. I couldn't wait to show it to Mitch. Seven kids from my fifth grade class had them. By the time we started the sixth grade, I bet even more would have them. Every bracelet had the name of a soldier who was either a prisoner of war or missing in action in Vietnam. The date they became missing or captured was also engraved on it.

You weren't supposed to take it off until the person on it came home from the war. Dead or alive.

Mom caught up, but I couldn't help running on ahead again. I was too excited.

As I got to the front of the terminal, I could hear yelling. About 20 teenagers wearing tie-dyed shirts and bell-bottom pants walked in a circle carrying home-made signs. The signs said things like BRING THE TROOPS HOME NOW!, GET OUT OF VIETNAM!, and SUPPOSE THEY HAD A WAR AND NOBODY CAME?

As they marched in a circle, they chanted, "Hell no, we won't go!"

They really made me mad. My brother had joined the Army. He was willing to risk his life to help some little country thousands of miles away be free. These guys had the nerve to say they'd refuse to go if they were drafted. Well, then, they'd have to run off to live in Canada.

I wished they'd go today. Why did they have to choose now to protest? Why did they have to choose the airport?

I tried to ignore them as I walked by.

"Hey, who's on your POW bracelet?" someone asked.

I looked up to see a skinny guy with frizzy red hair and glasses. I noticed he had on a bracelet, too. His bracelet had a little round white sticker with a blue star. That meant the soldier on his bracelet was MIA, missing in action. Mine had a blue sticker with a white star for POW, prisoner of war.

I knew the name and date on my bracelet by heart.

"Major Jack Tomes—7/7/66," I answered.

"Man," the guy said. "He's been a prisoner for over two years."

I turned to look for Mom. She was coming across the street.

"My soldier has only been MIA for six months," he said. He looked down at his own bracelet. "If they'd just stop this war, they could all come home. We never should have sent troops there in the first place."

"You don't know what you're talking about," I said. I was thinking about Maggie. "My best friend's dad died over there. She's proud that he died serving his country. He was trying to keep the world free."

"Maybe you don't know what you're talking about either," he said.

He handed me a bumper sticker with a peace symbol on it. I wadded it up and handed it to Emmett.

"This is for you," I said.

Emmett uncrumpled the sticker.

"Don't mind her," Emmett said. "She's too young to understand."

"You are!" I yelled. Emmett shrugged his shoulders and then held up two fingers in a peace sign.

"Keep up the good fight," Emmett said.

"Right on!" the guy answered, holding up his fist.

Mom and Lee Ann finally made it to the door. I pushed Mom inside before she had a chance to get in an argument with the protesters, too.

A cool blast of air hit us as we entered the terminal. We quickly looked at the flight schedule behind the ticket counter.

"Flight 782 from San Diego," I read out loud. "Arriving at gate A-27."

"Good heavens," Mom said. "His plane is on the ground already. And that gate is clear at the other end of the terminal."

"Let's run!" I said. "We can still make it in time to meet him."

"You go on ahead. I can't run in these shoes," she said. "I'll catch up."

"I'll stay with you, Mrs. Morgan," Lee Ann said. "I'm having a hard time in these platform shoes, too."

I grabbed Emmett's hand.

"Come on," I said. He didn't argue or pull his hand back. I knew that he missed Mitchell as much as any of us. Even if he didn't agree with the war.

We got to the gate just as a stewardess opened the door. Through the window, I could see people still coming down the stairs of the plane and across the tarmac.

"Do you see him?" I asked, jumping up and down. Emmett was six feet tall and had a better view.

The people standing in front of us walked away, one after the other. A couple of Marines walked past us. But where was Mitchell? Had he already walked by? Maybe I hadn't known him. Maybe he wouldn't know us, either. I was only ten the last time he saw me. I was practically a teenager now. And Emmett had grown at least six inches.

Emmett put his hands on my shoulders. It seemed like forever while we watched other passengers file into the airport. Finally, there was a tall, thin man wearing a green uniform in the doorway. He had a bag over his shoulder. His blond hair was cut Army-short.

His tanned face broke into a dimpled grin when he saw us.

"Mitch!" I yelled. I ran to him. He hugged me so hard I couldn't breathe.

"I missed you," he said. His voice sounded funny. He stood back and looked at me. "Sam, you sure did grow up in the last 13 months. I'll have to get a big stick to keep the boys away."

"I already have one," Emmett said.

"You guys be quiet," I said, but I was smiling.

"Sam, who's this hippie with you?" Mitch asked. He ruffled Emmett's long hair with his hand. "Don't tell me it's my baby brother!"

Emmett punched Mitch in the shoulder. Mitch grabbed him and hugged him. Emmett's face turned bright red, but he hugged him back.

"Where's Mom?" Mitch asked.

"She's coming with Lee Ann any minute," I said. "They've got on platforms and can't run so well."

"Lee Ann's here, too?" he asked.

"Mitch!" Lee Ann said, coming up beside us.

Mitch turned and hugged and kissed her all in one move. Then he noticed Mom waiting patiently.

"Now who is this beautiful lady?" he teased. "Lee Ann, I'm throwing you over for someone else."

Lee Ann laughed her dumb laugh. Mitch hugged Mom. This time it was Mitch who couldn't breathe.

"Oh, my boy is finally back," Mom said. "I never thought I'd see you again. I swear I didn't. So many boys come home in . . . in . . ."

"Shh, Mom," Mitch said. "I'm home now."

I knew what she was thinking. We'd seen the military planes landing with row after row of shiny aluminum coffins. Each one holding the body of a soldier killed in Vietnam. Each one someone's son, or husband, or father—or brother. One of them had held Maggie's dad.

9

I shuddered. I wasn't going to think about it. Mitch was safe now.

Mom and Mitch stood there hugging a while longer. People passed. Some smiled. Most just ignored us.

"Hey, Sam," Mitch said. "How about riding on my back like you used to?"

"Here?" I asked.

"Why not?" he said.

"I weigh too much now," I said.

"Heck, I carried more weight than you in 'Nam," he said.

I laughed and got on his back. We started down the hall.

"See, I told you. You're light as a feather."

I held tight to his strong shoulders. I never felt so happy to be with anyone as I did right then.

At that moment, for me, the war was over. My brother was back in the U.S. I was never going to think about Vietnam again.

# Baby Killer!

We got Mitchell's bags and headed to our car. The protesters were still standing near the doors. We were across the street before any of them noticed us.

"Hey, Baby Killer!"

At first I didn't understand. Baby killer? Who could they be talking to? Then another protester spoke up.

"We're talking to you, soldier," she said. "How many babies did you murder in Vietnam?"

She was talking to my brother. I couldn't believe it. How could she ask that? My brother went to Vietnam to fight the Communists. How could she think he killed babies?

Mitch stared at the protesters. His face had gone pale. He looked confused.

"You've got the wrong guy," he said. "I'm one of the good guys."

The protesters laughed. One or two of them spit on the ground.

"You're just a killer hired by Uncle Sam," one said.

"Take that back!" Mom yelled. "You're nothing but a bunch of dirty hippies. You wouldn't know a decent person if you saw one." Mom started across the street toward the group. Her face was red and her fists were clenched. I couldn't wait to see her hit a few of those teenagers.

Mitch grabbed Mom's shoulder.

"Let it go, Mom," Mitch said. "I just want to go home."

Lee Ann stood close to both of them. Two tears slid down her cheeks. Mitch rubbed his eyes and then put on his sunglasses.

"Let's go, Mrs. Morgan," Lee Ann whispered.

Mom didn't move.

"Mom, if I get in a fight, I'll probably get arrested," Mitch said. "You don't want me to spend my first day back in the U.S. in jail, do you?"

I looked at the protesters, who had started chanting, "Killer, killer, killer!" I didn't know who I was madder

at—them or Emmett. He was pretending he didn't know us.

"I'll hit them," I said. "The police won't arrest me."

"I didn't come all this way to see my baby sister get into a fight," Mitch said. "Be cool."

"Then just let me hit Emmett," I said.

"What did I do?" Emmett asked.

*Splat!* An egg landed on the ground in front of us. Then another. A beer bottle crashed on the sidewalk near us.

"Let's go," Mitch said.

We all walked quickly away.

Finally, we reached the parking garage. I slipped my hand into Mitch's free hand as we started up the steps. Lee Ann went back to walk with Mom up the stairs.

"I'm sorry those peaceniks ruined your homecoming," I said.

He squeezed my hand and cleared his throat. Then he noticed my POW bracelet.

"What's this?" he asked.

I told him about it.

"I like that," he said. "Maybe I'll get one, too." He frowned as he looked back at Lee Ann.

"Skirts sure got shorter while I was gone," he said. "I hope you don't have any that short."

"I have a couple," I said. "But mostly I wear jeans."

"Good," he said. Then he whispered, "I don't think

I like that white lipstick Lee Ann's got on much either. It makes her look . . ."

"Creepy?" I asked.

Mitch laughed.

"Something like that," he said. "But I suppose that's the latest thing, too, right?"

I nodded. "It's groovy."

We finally made it to the car. Emmett unlocked the trunk.

"Put your bag in the trunk, G. I. Joe," Emmett said to Mitch. I shot a worried look at Mom. She closed her eyes. I could tell she was counting to ten.

Mitch smiled. "Do you still have your G. I. Joe, with all his gear?" he asked. "He used to be your favorite toy."

Emmett shook his head. "I threw him out," he said. "I don't believe in war toys. Or war."

"Sometimes it's the only way," Mitch said. He looked right into Emmett's eyes. Mitch was always doing that. I always felt like he could read my mind when he stared at me that way. It drove me crazy.

Emmett stared back. He jingled the car keys in his pocket. Finally, Mitch broke the silence.

"Don't tell me you're going to drive?"

Emmett's face broke into a wide grin. He dangled the keys in front of Mitch's face.

"That's right," he said in a singsongy voice.

Mitch made a grab for the keys. Emmett pulled the keys away and jumped into the driver's seat. We all piled into the car. Mom and I sat in the back. Lee Ann got to sit up front between Mitch and Emmett.

The car started on the third try. Mitch was the only one who put on his seat belt. Lee Ann laughed.

Emmett ground the gears and pulled the car out of the parking space. The tires squealed as he drove toward the exit.

"I hope you have insurance!" Mitch yelled above the engine.

"Nope," Emmett said. "It's a risk when you drive with me."

Mitch shook his head and covered his eyes with his hands.

"I felt safer in Vietnam," he said.

Everyone laughed. But, after Mitch's welcome from the protesters, I wasn't really sure he was joking.

# Nightmares
# and Memories

In the morning, I went downstairs to find Mom in her usual hurry to get to work. She was tying her apron around her waist.

"I thought you had today off," I said.

"Sally called in sick," Mom said. "Carol called me in a panic. The Lion's Club is having their monthly lunch meeting in the dining room. She begged me to come and help her."

Carol was Mom's boss at the Steak and Shrimp

Restaurant. She was always calling Mom in a panic about something.

"Where's Mitch?" I asked.

"Still asleep," Mom said. "He hasn't slept in a couple of days. I'll probably be back before he wakes up. If he does wake up, tell him to call Lee Ann. She's already called twice."

Mom stopped and looked at me.

"See if Mitch will talk to you about Vietnam, too," she said.

"Why?"

"Because he told me he wasn't ready to talk about it yet. Said he might never be ready," she said. "And then he said I wouldn't understand anyway. How could his mother not understand?"

"I can't make him tell me stuff he doesn't want to," I said.

"Try," Mom said. Then she grabbed her purse and ran out the back door.

Emmett was sitting at the kitchen table, painting on a big piece of cardboard. I looked over his shoulder. He had penciled in what he was going to paint. It said, "War is not healthy for children and other living things."

I didn't know what children had to do with war. But I didn't say anything. I didn't feel like arguing with Emmett.

"What's your sign for?" I asked.

"The Die-In tomorrow," he said.

Hippies were always having "Ins" of some sort. Last summer they had a "Be-In" at the park. It was supposed to be a celebration of life—a party. They listened to loud music, danced, and some people even took drugs. I didn't know what a Die-In was, though.

"Die-In?"

"People get dressed up like Vietnamese people. Then they cover themselves with fake blood and lie in the streets."

"What for?"

"It's supposed to show how terrible this war is for the people of Vietnam. The people we're supposedly trying to save."

"Soldiers are fighting the war," I said, "not regular people."

"Who do you think all the bombs get dropped on? Do you think the soldiers check first to see if there are any innocent people among the Viet Cong?"

"Oh, shut up," I muttered. But he'd gotten me thinking. I'd watched the six o'clock news every night during dinner with Mom and Emmett. Most of the time there was film of soldiers firing their guns into the trees. Or running for cover. Sometimes there were pictures of injured Vietnamese people, but I'd never thought that our soldiers might be responsible.

"Sometimes people who look innocent *are* the Viet Cong." Emmett and I both looked up. Mitch was standing in the kitchen doorway in gym shorts and no shirt.

"So what do you do?" Emmett asked. "Shoot first? Ask questions later?"

Mitch opened the refrigerator and took out a quart of milk. He slammed the door so hard the Coca-Cola bottles clinked against each other inside.

"No, we usually wait until some kid throws a grenade at us. We like to make sure one or two of our guys get killed before we do anything. We can't have people like you thinking we're bad."

Having Mitch home wasn't supposed to be like this. My dad died before I was born. Mitch used to take care of me when Mom was at work. He cooked dinner for me and Emmett. He took us to high school football games and fishing in Dobbs Pond. Mitch was as much a father as a brother to me. I was supposed to be really happy he was here. But I wasn't feeling happy now.

Emmett bent over his sign again. "Everything about this war is bad," he said.

"I hope you mean the Viet Cong, too," Mitch said.

"I don't know," Emmett said. "Are they really the enemy? They are just Vietnamese people who want Communism in their country and are willing to fight for it."

"And what about the people who don't want Communism?" Mitch asked. "What about the people who want to own land, and not share everything with the

20

government? People who want to be able to say what they please."

Emmett shrugged.

"There are plenty of people who are against Ho Chi Minh's Communist movement," Mitch went on. "Although he's trying to kill them off as fast as he can."

"You mean he is killing his own people?" I asked. I twisted the bracelet on my wrist. If they would do that to their own people, what would they do to POWs?

Mitch nodded. "The Viet Cong kill any villagers who won't help them," he said. "Sometimes they wipe out whole villages—women, children, everyone. Even the pets."

Emmett looked up. "U.S. troops never do that, of course," he said. He shook his head. "Pretty soon all the people we are supposed to save will be dead."

I thought for a minute that Mitch was going to hit Emmett. He didn't. He turned and went back upstairs. He didn't even slam the door to his room.

"Emmett," I said. "Can't you keep your mouth shut?"

"If people like me keep our mouths shut, this war is going to go on forever," he said.

I sighed. Did he really believe he was going to change anything? Couldn't he just be glad his brother was home?

I poured myself a glass of milk and started to leave.

"Sam." Emmett said. "In two years, I'll be 18. The

government will be able to draft me into the army then. Do you really want me to go to Vietnam, too?"

I swallowed hard. Of course I didn't. I shook my head. Emmett dipped his brush into some red paint.

"I'm not as smart as Mitch," he said. "I'd get myself wasted the first day there. That's my worst nightmare."

"Wasted?" I asked.

"Killed," he said. "Zapped. Blown away. Any way you look at it, I'd be dead. And there will be thousands more just like me if the war doesn't stop."

I sighed and went upstairs. Mitch was lying on his bed in his room. He looked like he was already asleep again. I tiptoed over and stared down at him. I was so glad he was alive and home. Maybe after he came back from the base in North Carolina, we would all get along better—like we used to.

I didn't know how he could be asleep with the windows wide open like they were. The sun was streaming down on him and the birds outside were making a racket.

I walked over to the window to close the shades. As I pulled the shade down, I noticed some photographs on his dresser. The color wasn't very good. There were several pictures of a guy with brown hair and freckles. There were also several pictures of Mitch and the same guy. I turned them over to see if Mitch had written who the person was on the back.

"That's my best friend, Jim Smith," Mitch said.

I jumped. His voice startled me.

"Sorry," I said. I laid the pictures back on his dresser.

"It's okay," he said. "I left them out to show you later. He and his wife are going to come and visit me as soon as he gets back to the world."

"He's still in Vietnam?" I asked.

Mitch nodded.

"Jim's quite a guy," he said smiling. "He saved me a couple of times. He also has more funny stories to tell than anyone I've ever known. He says it's because he's a Texan."

"Are you worried about him?" I asked.

"Yeah, I am," he said. "He's the best friend I've ever had. I'm always thinking about him. He's short, though, so he should be home soon."

"Why? Do they get sent home sooner if they're short?" I asked.

Mitch laughed.

"Short means he has a short time left in-country— in 'Nam. He only has 3 or 4 more weeks to go."

"He looks like a nice guy," I said.

"You'll get to meet him soon," Mitch said.

"Think he'd tell me one of his stories?" I asked.

"Sure," Mitch said. He sighed. "I wish I wasn't so tired."

Mitch hadn't opened his eyes the whole time he was talking to me. In a minute, he was snoring softly. I stood beside the bed watching him. A car drove by with a noisy engine. It backfired three times right in front of our house—*pop, pop, pop.*

Suddenly, Mitch's eyes snapped open. He reached his right arm out quickly and fell off the bed. He knocked me over as he rolled onto his stomach. The empty glass in my hand flew across the room and shattered against the wall. My POW bracelet cut into my wrist as I hit the floor.

It was over in a matter of seconds. Mitch still covered his head with his left arm. His right arm was out in front of him as if he were reaching for something. My heart was pounding right in my ears.

Mitch slowly lifted his head to look at me. A sheepish grin spread across his face.

"Sorry, Sam," he said. "I forgot where I was for a minute. I was going for my rifle."

I sat next to him, rubbing my wrist.

"I know where *I* was for a minute," I said. "Vietnam. It must have been a horrible place to be."

Mitch got up and the floor squeaked in front of his bed. He put his foot down and made it squeak again. Then he helped me up. We both sat on his bed.

"Thinking about this house is what got me through my tour," he said. "I couldn't wait to be home. I knew I could feel safe in a place where I know every squeak in every floor—and every hole and crack in the walls."

He rubbed a long crack in the wall behind his bed. "I couldn't wait to be in a place where there were no surprises."

He laughed.

"Here I am at last and I'm still jumping at every noise."

"It's okay," I said. "I guess it will take you a while to get used to being home."

"Maybe forever," he said. He lay down and closed his eyes again. "I was so happy to be coming home."

I stared down at him for a minute more. Then I tiptoed from his room and closed the door.

# A Die-In

"We already know which brother you side with," Emmett said. "So it won't hurt you to go to the Die-In with me."

"Would you quit bugging me about going?" I asked.

I was curious about the Die-In—what Emmett and his friends were planning. It was sure to get in the newspaper. But I wasn't sure I should go. I didn't think Mitch would like it.

"You just don't want to see what the war is really like," Emmett said.

"As if you know what it's like!" Mitch yelled from the living room. He and Lee Ann were watching soap operas or something on TV.

"I watch the news. I've seen what's going on over there!" Emmett yelled back.

"What makes you think they are showing you the whole story?" Mitch asked. He came into the kitchen. He took two Cokes from the fridge.

All the yelling was giving me a headache. I wished they would stop.

"You're just afraid your little sister will start going to peace marches if she finds out what the war is really like. You're worried I might talk her into thinking the war should end."

"I *do* want the war to end," I said. Mitch stopped and looked at me. Emmett smiled. I went on, "I want all the soldiers to come home." I held up my arm with my bracelet on it.

"I want Major Jack Tomes 7/7/66 to come home to his family. I want the killing to stop. But I don't want North Vietnam—the Communists—to win."

Mitch smiled, too.

"It sounds like our little sister has a mind of her own," he said. "She doesn't need us to tell her how to think."

"Of course she doesn't," Lee Ann said. She took a Coke from Mitch. "If you guys weren't arguing all the time, you might have noticed before now."

I smiled at Lee Ann.

"So, Sam," Emmett asked. "Are you going to come with me or not?"

I looked at Mitch. I didn't want to make him mad.

"Lee Ann and I will drop you off on our way downtown," he said.

"Do *you* think I should go?" I asked.

Mitch stared right into my eyes. I looked down at the floor.

"I don't think *I* should go," Mitch said. "But you have to make your own choice. No one can do that for you."

"Call one of your friends," Emmett said. "Get someone to go with you."

"Right," I said. "Who am I going to call, Maggie? She'd love going to hear how her dad died for nothing."

"You don't have to call Maggie. What about Sara?"

"She'll probably be there anyway," I said. "Marching with her brother. She's nice, but kind of weird."

"Well?" Mitch asked. He was staring at me again.

"Okay," I said. "I would like to see what a Die-In is like. Even though it sounds kind of stupid to me."

Emmett picked up his sign.

"Let's go," he said.

We drove downtown and Mitch let us out in front of the library.

"We'll come back for you in a couple of hours," Mitch said.

"Be careful," Lee Ann said to me. I didn't know why she said that. It wasn't a real war.

Emmett and I walked to the city hall a block away. When we got there, a big group was already chanting "Out of Vietnam now!" Sara was there carrying a doll with an arm missing.

"I'm so glad you're here," she said.

"I just came to watch," I said quickly.

Emmett shook hands with her brother, Tom.

"Hey man," Emmett said. "Did you bring the blood?"

"Got it right here," Tom said. He held up a paper sack. It was from the costume shop around the corner. He pulled out a plastic bottle full of red liquid. He gave it to Emmett.

"Squeeze this on me," Emmett said. He handed me the bottle.

I aimed the bottle at Emmett's chest and squeezed. Thick red liquid ran down his front.

"I'm hit!" Emmett yelled. He clutched his chest. His hand came back covered in fake blood. It looked horrible.

"Hit me again."

I squeezed out more. That was when I noticed my hand shaking.

"Put some on me," Sara said.

I handed the bottle back to Tom. "Here," I said. "You do this."

I turned and tried to make my way through the crowd. My stomach felt tight. I hit my knee on something hard.

"Ouch!"

"Sorry," a man said.

I looked down to see a man in a wheelchair. He was looking up at me. He had on a faded Army shirt. He didn't have any legs.

At first I thought he might be one of the actors in the Die-In—that somehow his legs were hidden. But he was real.

"Are you okay?" he asked.

I nodded.

"I want to watch from across the street in the park," he said. "Could you help me get my chair over there?"

I nodded again and got behind his chair and pushed. There were lots of people in the way. When we made it to the street, cars were parked across the crosswalk. People in their cars were stopping to stare.

I finally parked the chair on top of a small hill in the park beside a bench. I sat down.

"Thanks," he said.

The protesters were still chanting. I'd seen this before. Weren't they going to do anything different?

"Were you in Vietnam?" I asked the man. I knew the answer. He looked down where his legs used to be.

"Part of me is still there," he said, laughing. I didn't laugh. It didn't seem funny to me at all.

"My brother just got back from Vietnam," I said. "He's home on leave. My other brother is over there." I pointed at the crowd across the street.

"How does your brother like being home?" he asked.

For a minute, I didn't know what to say. I thought about the protesters at the airport, about the arguments with Emmett. I thought about the squeaking floor and the car backfiring.

"He's getting used to it," I said.

"He's probably really missing Vietnam about now," he said.

"You're crazy," I said. "He doesn't miss Vietnam."

"Trust me. He probably had a lot of friends there. Men he could count on. Men who understood exactly what he'd been through."

"Do you miss Vietnam?" I asked.

"I did at first," he said. "I told you, part of me is still there. And I don't mean my legs."

"What do you mean?"

"Going to Vietnam changed my whole life. The kid who went over isn't the same person who came back."

I nodded. It was the same with Mitchell. He was different, too. He was quieter. He didn't joke around like he used to. He used to tell us everything about his life. Now it seemed like he had lots of secrets.

"When I first got back, it was terrible. People didn't know what to say to me. So they didn't say anything

at all. It was like they were trying to ignore the whole war. It's better now, though."

"How did it get better?"

"I have some friends to talk to at the Veterans Hospital," he said. "Friends help."

Across the street, someone started hitting a drum. It sounded like gun shots. People started screaming and falling to the ground.

Sara yelled, "My baby, my baby! Don't hurt my baby!"

I knew it was all a big show, but it looked and sounded real. In the distance, I heard police sirens.

"The police are coming to break it up," the man said. "They will say we are disturbing the peace."

He laughed again.

"More like disturbing the war," he said. "I hope your brother doesn't get arrested."

"Arrested?" I was surprised.

"If the protesters don't leave, the police will arrest them."

"I've got to find my brother," I said.

"I enjoyed talking to you." He held out his hand. I shook it.

"Be patient with your brothers," he said. "Both of them. They have a lot on their minds."

I waved to him and ran across the street to find Emmett. When I got to the other side, I ran right into Mitch and Lee Ann.

"We've got to get Emmett and leave, " I said breathlessly.

"We know," Lee Ann said. "Your mom would have a fit if he gets arrested."

The protesters were walking in a circle and chanting "Out of Vietnam now!"

I grabbed Emmett when he went by and pulled him out of line.

"Time to go home," I said. Emmett pulled away from me.

"No way, man. I'm staying."

"You're going to get arrested," I said.

"So," he said. "I believe in this."

"You had your Die-In," Lee Ann said. "You've made your stand. What's the point in getting arrested?"

"I don't expect you to understand," Emmett said.

"Come on, man," Mitch said. "Don't be a hero. You did what you came to do. Let's go home."

Emmett stopped for a minute. The sirens were louder. People were starting to scatter. He nodded and we all ran down the street toward the library parking lot.

"I feel like a deserter," Emmett said.

Mitch put his arm around his shoulders.

"But at least you won't be sentenced to five years of hard labor," Mitch said. "Which is what Mom would have given if you'd gotten yourself arrested."

Emmett smiled and put his arm around Mitch's shoulders.

"I owe you my life," Emmett said.

Lee Ann laughed. She held Mitch's hand and I held Emmett's. It was the first time since the airport that Mitch and Emmett had acted like they cared about each other. It was beautiful.

# Wasted

"These are the voyages of the starship, *Enterprise* . . ."
We were all sitting in our living room with the lights
out, watching *Star Trek*. Mom sat beside Mitch on the
couch. Lee Ann sat on the other side of him. Emmett
and I sat in the chair together.

This was a big night. Mitch had never seen *Star Trek*
before. He said lots of guys just getting to Vietnam
had told him what a neat show it was.

It was a rerun, but I didn't care. It was my favorite

show—Emmett's, too. It was the only show we didn't argue about.

By the time the first commercial came on, Mitch was hooked.

"Man, I wish we'd had some of those phasers in 'Nam," he said. "We could have used guns like that." Then he laughed. "Or better yet, that transporter. Beam me up. I'm surrounded."

Always Vietnam. He always said just enough to get Emmett going. Never enough to tell us much about it. Every time the subject came up, I held my breath waiting for Emmett to start yelling and Mitch to start yelling back.

I just wanted them to talk about something else. Mitch was home and the war would be over before Emmett could get drafted. Good grief! They were going to put men in orbit around the moon by Christmas. If they were smart enough to do that, Mom said, they could surely figure out how to stop the war in Vietnam.

The war was over for us, I repeated to myself. The bracelet on my wrist reflected the light from the TV into my eyes. I looked down at my arm. *Major Jack Tomes 7/7/66.* Almost over, anyway.

"Sam, get that cake I brought home from work," Mom said. "Mitch probably needs a snack."

Mitch grinned at Mom. I got up and went to the kitchen.

"I'll help you," Lee Ann said. I got plates and forks, while Lee Ann got napkins and the cake.

"Sam, does Mitch talk to you?" she asked suddenly. "I mean about the war?"

I didn't answer. She went on quickly. "He seems so different. Quieter. He doesn't seem happy. I want to help, but I don't know how."

I felt sorry for her. Mitch would always be my brother—even if he didn't talk to me. He didn't always have to be her boyfriend.

"He hasn't said much," I said. "But I know it was scary over there. He might miss Vietnam, too." I told her about the car backfiring and what the man with no legs said.

"Do you think he'll ever act like his old self again?" she asked.

"I don't know," I said.

We started to leave the kitchen.

"Hey, what's this?" she asked. She pointed to an envelope lying on the counter.

It was a letter to Mitch. It was addressed to Corporal Mitchell Morgan. The return address said it was from Linda Smith in Texas. It wasn't opened.

Lee Ann picked up the letter.

"I think Corporal Morgan has some explaining to do," she said.

Lee Ann set the cake down hard on the coffee table. She threw the letter at Mitch.

"Mail call!" she said.

Mitch looked surprised. Before he looked at the letter, Mom spoke up.

"Oh, I forgot to give that to you," she said. "It came in today's mail."

Mitch read the envelope and his face broke into a wide grin.

"It's from Jim's wife," he said. "She's planning their trip."

"Who's Jim?" Lee Ann asked.

"His best friend," I said. "He's coming to visit Mitch when he gets back from Vietnam."

Lee Ann turned red up to the tips of her ears. Mitch opened the letter while he watched the show. Mom cut him a piece of cake. He put the letter down to take his cake. After the next commercial, he picked it up to read it.

Lee Ann, Emmett, and Mom were so busy watching Captain Kirk that they didn't notice Mitch. I did. His face got very white. He rubbed his eyes two or three times. Then he got up and walked out onto the front porch.

Through the screen door, I could see him sit down. The letter was crumpled in his hand. Something was wrong.

I went outside. Mitch didn't move an inch when I came out and sat beside him. He was staring at the ground. The crickets were chirping. The teenagers

next door were playing "Hey Jude" by The Beatles on their stereo.

"Mitch?" I asked. I didn't have to say more.

"It's Jim," he said. He rubbed his eyes again. "He got wasted in Vietnam—the day after I left."

Mitch sighed and his body shuddered like he was cold.

"The jeep Jim was riding in hit a land mine. Everyone with him was killed, too."

"I'm sorry," I said.

Mitch didn't look at me. He didn't even seem to hear me. He got up and started pacing. He walked out to the gate and back to the front porch. He did it again and again.

Finally he stopped. He stuck his hands in his back pockets.

"I've got to go," he said. "Get the car keys for me, would you?"

"Go where?" I asked.

"Anywhere. Nowhere. Somewhere," he said. "Please, Sam, get me the keys."

I got the keys. Mom and Lee Ann looked up when I passed through the living room. I didn't say anything.

I handed the keys to Mitch. Lee Ann came outside.

"Where are we going?" she asked. Mitch didn't answer. He walked quickly to the car, got in, and started the engine.

"What's going on, Sam?" Lee Ann asked me. Emmett and Mom stood behind her.

"Jim got wasted in Vietnam," I said.

"Oh, Lord," Mom said.

Mitch started to pull the car out of the driveway.

"Wait!" Lee Ann yelled. Mitch slammed on the brakes. Lee Ann ran to the passenger side and jumped into the car. Mitch never looked at her as they drove off down the road.

I was jealous that Lee Ann was the one who got to try and make him feel better. But I didn't think I'd know what to say to him anyway.

"Wasted," Emmett repeated angrily. "What a perfect word."

# Going Back

Mitch was even quieter for a few days after he got the news about Jim. Then suddenly he seemed happier. Everyone noticed the change. I decided that Lee Ann must have said the right things to him. But she seemed sadder. I wondered if they were going to break up when he went to North Carolina.

One morning, Mom sent me to the corner store for milk. I hurried on the way back. I wanted to watch *The Dating Game* on TV.

I heard crying and yelling before I even got to our

house. I hurried up the front steps. Emmett almost knocked me down as he came out of the house.

"You're an idiot, Mitch!" he yelled over his shoulder.

Mom was upstairs. I could hear her crying. She was supposed to be at work soon. I heard Mitch's soft voice talking to her. I heard Lee Ann, too. Mom was saying, "Please, please."

Outside, Emmett honked the horn.

I stood at the bottom of the steps. I wasn't sure what to do. What was happening? Had Mitch and Emmett finally gotten into a fist fight?

I heard Mom's footsteps coming down. She blew her nose.

"What's going on, Mom?" I asked.

She started crying again. Then she hugged me.

"He says he's leaving, honey," she said. "Go up and try to talk some sense into him—please. He won't listen to me."

Mom sat down hard on the couch. Why was she so upset about Mitch leaving a few days early? My stomach hurt as I walked slowly upstairs.

Mitch's door was open. Lee Ann was watching him pack. He had his back to me. I tapped lightly on the open door.

"Come on in, Sam," he said. He didn't turn around.

He had on his uniform. I felt a lump in my throat.

"How come you're leaving early?" I asked. "I thought you still had a few more days on your leave."

"I'm going to go see Jim's wife in Texas," he said. "You know I can fly free any place in the U.S. if I wear my uniform."

"When do you have to be in North Carolina?" I asked. I twisted my bracelet around and around on my wrist.

"I'm not going to the base in North Carolina," he said.

I knew what question I should ask. But I couldn't. I didn't want to know the answer.

"Do you think you'll get to come home for Christmas?"

Mitch shook his head. He stared right into my eyes. I wished he wouldn't do that. I looked away.

"Then come home for Thanksgiving. We'll have your presents for you early."

"I'm going back to Vietnam," he said.

I put my hands over my ears.

"Don't say it," I said. "I won't listen. You can't go back!"

Lee Ann stood up and put her arm around me. I pushed her away.

"How could you let him do this?" I yelled at her. "If he was my boyfriend, I sure wouldn't let him go off to war if he didn't have to."

"Sam, listen to me," Mitch said. "I made up my own mind. I want to go back."

"Why?"

Mitch sighed.

"It's Emmett and the other protesters," I said. "That's why you're going back, isn't it?"

"Don't blame Emmett for this, Sam."

"I will if I want to!"

Mitch put an arm around me. I twisted away.

"Sam, I learned a lot in Vietnam. Not just about how to fight, but about myself, too. War can bring out the worst in people, but it can also bring out the best. That's what it did for me."

He put his hand on my shoulder and went on.

"I made great friends in Vietnam. Better than any I'll ever have again. They were men I could count on for anything and everything. I like the way it feels to have friends like that."

I kept my back to him. But in the mirror I could see him look at Lee Ann. She shrugged.

"Heck, Sam, maybe I can train some new grunts. Teach them how to stay alive."

"I want *you* to stay alive."

Mitch zipped his suitcase without saying anything.

"Mom needs you," I said. "How can you do this to her?"

"She has you and Emmett," he said. "And I'll be back."

"When?"

Mitch didn't answer. He carried his stuff out of the room and down the stairs. Lee Ann and I followed close behind.

Mom was still on the couch crying. I turned away when she looked up at me. Lee Ann went to sit beside her.

"Mrs. Morgan," she said. "Please try to understand how Mitch feels. He has to go back."

"Why?" she said. "So I can spend another year worrying every minute?"

Mitch sat down beside Mom and hugged her.

Emmett slammed in the front door.

"I suppose you expect me to take you to the airport," Emmett said. "Forget it. I'm not taking you to your own funeral."

"Lee Ann, will you and Sam wait outside a minute?" Mitch asked. "I need to talk with Mom and Emmett."

Lee Ann and I sat on the back porch. For the first time, I noticed how red Lee Ann's eyes were. She'd already done her crying. She held my hand tightly.

I could hear angry voices inside, but I couldn't hear what they were saying. I wished they would stop. I didn't want Mitch to remember us this way. I didn't want him to think I thought the war was wrong. Or that his choice to fight was wrong. I just wanted it to be over. I wanted my brother safe.

Mitch came out and put his bags in the trunk of

the car. Emmett came out, blowing his nose. He opened the driver's side door and got in.

"Come and see me off at the airport," Mitch said. "I don't want this ugly hippie to be the only one waving good-bye."

Emmett smiled weakly. Lee Ann shook her head.

"I'll stay here with your mom," she said. Mitch hugged her.

"Write me every day," he said.

She pressed her lips tightly together and nodded.

I got in the front seat between Mitch and Emmett. We rode in silence all the way. No one even bothered to turn on the radio.

"Just drop me at the terminal," Mitch said. "It will be better that way."

I looked for any signs of protesters. I didn't see any.

Emmett stopped the car. He handed Mitch the keys to unlock the trunk. Emmett didn't move from his seat. I got out with Mitch.

I didn't know what to say. What could I say?

"Be careful" sounded dumb. The Viet Cong shot careful soldiers all the time. "Come home soon?" That sounded stupid, too.

"I love you," I blurted out. Mitch stopped taking the last bag from the trunk. He stared at me for a minute, then grabbed me in a bear hug.

"I love you, too, Samantha Morgan," he said. "I already miss you."

Emmett got out of the car. He held out his hand to shake Mitch's hand.

"Don't be a hero, okay?" Emmett said.

"Too late," I said. "He's already a hero." Mitch stared right into my eyes the way he always did. This time I didn't look away.

Mitch shook Emmett's hand then, and gave him the same bear hug he'd given me. Then he picked up his bags and walked inside.

Emmett and I stood there and watched him go. After a while, we couldn't see him in the crowd anymore.

## ABOUT THIS BOOK

The 1960s were a time of change. Many things were new—the hairstyles, the clothes, the music, the increase in illegal drug use. And young people everywhere were deciding which of the changes were important in their own lives. They were making choices.

President Lyndon Johnson thought it was important for the United States to send troops to Vietnam. He wanted to stop Communism from spreading. Many Americans agreed. Others thought we should not get involved. They thought it was a waste of lives.

Many men were excused from going to Vietnam. Some, like Mitch, volunteered to go. Others simply went because they thought it was their only choice. Still others chose to go to jail, or move to Canada, to avoid Vietnam.

In 1968, when this book takes place, I was 13 years old. I was living in a small town in Oklahoma. Just like Sam, I wore a POW bracelet with the name *Maj. Jack Tomes 7/7/66* engraved on it. (He returned to the United States in 1973—seven years after his capture.)

At my school, a girl who was a year younger than I had a brother who went to Vietnam. One day, the girl came to school in tears. She told us her brother had been wounded—he might die. But he didn't die. He came home and became a basketball coach at our school. He told us many stories about Vietnam and how it had changed him.

No one in my town ever protested the war. But we saw the protests every night when we watched the news. It seemed that people all over America were deciding that the war was wrong.

Unfortunately, the people protesting the war often said and did terrible things to soldiers coming back from Vietnam. Many men were given worse "welcome homes" than the one I describe for Mitch. Soldiers were spit on. They had garbage thrown at them. They were told they should have died in Vietnam.

By the end of 1968, more than 31,000 U.S. soldiers had died in Vietnam. In 1973, when the peace treaties were signed, more than 58,000 Americans had been killed there.

Only recently, in 1982, were those Americans honored. A memorial was erected in Washington, D.C. It is a black granite wall 246 feet long. The name of each person who died or is missing in Vietnam is carved on it. It is a monument to those who served their country during a time of great change and tough choices.

N.A.